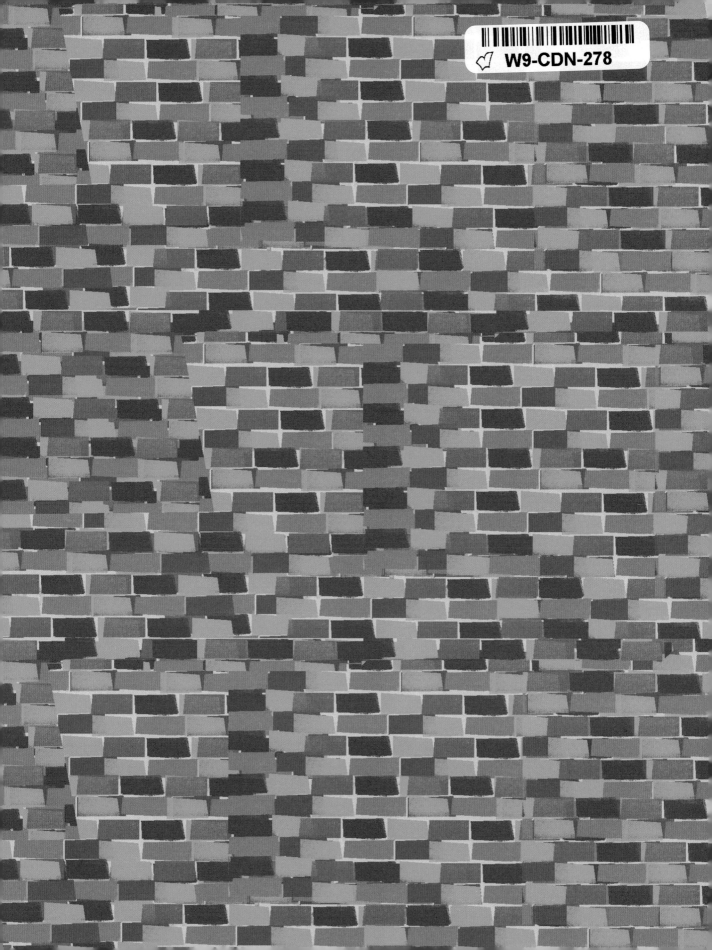

My Sister, Daisy

by Adria Karlsson   illustrated by Linus Curci

CAPSTONE EDITIONS
a capstone imprint

I was still very small when you were born.
You were scrunchy and tiny, and I loved you.
I don't remember a time when you weren't there.

I loved finding my favorite toys to show you.
I'd lie next to you as you batted at the toys dangling
down. I'd giggle and be silly, grabbing at them too.

You didn't know how to giggle yet, but you watched me.
I knew you thought I was funny.

I couldn't wait for us to play together.

As you got bigger, I pushed you in our little wagon
and helped you learn to eat. I loved to look at picture
books with you, snuggled up under a blanket.

We learned how to raise caterpillars into butterflies and how to pump our legs on the swings. I learned how to ride a bike.

We were brothers and best friends.

But then something changed. . . .

One day, the summer after you finished kindergarten,
you told me you were a girl.

I knew you wore dresses sometimes, but I thought it was because they were fun to twirl in.

I knew you were friends with girls, but so was I.

I knew you'd asked Mom to grow your hair long. But everyone knows long hair doesn't make someone a girl.

"Are you sure you're a girl?" I asked. "I have a friend who is a boy *and* a girl. They told us to use 'they' and 'them.'"

"I'm sure. I'm a girl! I'll use *she* and *her*," you declared. "Mom and Dad thought I was a boy when I was born, but they were wrong. I know who I am, and I *know* I'm a girl."

"Is it just playing with girls that makes you want to be called a girl?" I asked.

"Nope. That's not it," you said. "I don't want to be *called* a girl. I *am* a girl."

I guess it made sense. I *knew* I was a boy. I didn't have to think about it. I figured it must be the same for you. If you knew you were a girl, you *knew* it.

"Do you have a new name?" Dad asked.

"Yes! My name is Daisy, like the flower, because flowers are beautiful. I want a beautiful name," you said.

"Thanks for telling us," said Dad.
And, with a smile, he added, ". . . Daisy."

Thinking about it in the dark, quiet of my room, though, it felt a bit bigger and scarier than when you told me.

I was worried that you would change. I wasn't used to calling you Daisy.

"What if I forget?" I asked Dad quietly.

"We'll help you remember," he assured me.

I was afraid to call you by a new name and afraid to not have a brother anymore. I was afraid it meant losing you.

But . . . I tried it.

One week passed. Then another. I started to get used to having a sister!

I realized that you were still the same person, and we could play all the same games. We still had fun!

I helped other kids remember too. Mom and Dad got picture books from the library about kids like you. We talked to other families like ours. I learned the word *transgender*.

In the fall, we went back to school. Sometimes we joined the Rainbow Kids lunch, which was fun. Some kids came from families with two moms or two dads. Some were transgender or had questions about their gender or identity.

I met bigger kids who were transgender and more kids who weren't *he* or *she*.

I was proud to be your big brother. I tried to always use *she* and *her* and *sister* and *Daisy*.

Some days I didn't think about it at all. Some days I thought it was cool.

But some days I felt frustrated with myself when I said the wrong name for you. Some days I felt jealous that you got new clothes and lots of attention.

Sometimes jealous and angry feel the same. But I wasn't angry with *you*.

"Daisy gets all the attention now," I'd sometimes tell Mom. "I miss when she was my brother."

"But she's always been your sister," Mom would say. "Daisy is the same person. And now we understand what to call her and who she is inside."

"Sometimes people pay more attention to things that seem new," Dad added. "But that won't last forever. People will accept Daisy as she is, and that special attention will fade."

That helped me feel better. And they reminded me that I was special too.

Sometimes I think back to the days when I thought you were my brother. But now I love you as my sister.

We still ride bikes, play music, watch TV, and draw comics together.

Now, you're my sister, Daisy.

And you'll always be my best friend.

A Note from the Author

Just before my daughter turned six, while reading a bedtime story, she told me she was a girl. This was surprising as I had always assumed her to be my son. The book we were reading discussed gender identity and the gender spectrum—how the idea of boy versus girl doesn't work for everyone—and mentioned that the gender people are assigned at birth might not match who they are inside. But it is up to each person to determine and share their own identity.

My daughter told me that was her—she was a girl inside. I responded with something noncommittal and mostly attributed it to her connecting with the book. Over the next few months, she continued to be her bright and bubbly self. She also continued to dress in every type of clothing and was thrilled when her hair grew long enough to need headbands and clips. I did begin to wonder where she might fall on the gender spectrum. But I knew that gender expression was not necessarily tied to a person's gender identity. My child could present as a girl in terms of clothing and hairstyles, but still use male pronouns and be a boy. She had not mentioned being a girl again, and I was not ready to jump to any conclusions.

When kindergarten let out for the summer and camp began, my daughter told us that when asked for names and pronouns, she was going to say "she/her." This was the first time she had mentioned it since we read the book. We were surprised but supportive. Once camp started, she was thrilled with her new identity and asked us to use those pronouns at home too. We told her we could try it out. And when we asked her if she had a new name, without skipping a beat, she said her new name was "Rose, like the flowers, because flowers are beautiful."

As happy as Rose was with this change, it became obvious that her older brother was struggling. He and his sister were only fifteen months apart and had been treated as a pair of brothers for their entire lives. It was *this* change—the change in his identity—that seemed most difficult for him. His suggestion that Rose might be non-binary, both a boy and a girl, seemed to come from a place of trying to temper that change.

When I went looking for literature to support my son in his new role as "brother to a transgender sister," I found it lacking. When a sibling was present in a picture book about gender transition, they teased or questioned the legitimacy of the change, even if they eventually learned to accept it. I didn't want my son to see the wrong models in these stories or assume he was the "bad guy" in our story.

That is what inspired me to write this book—our family's story. While Daisy and her bravery in expressing her gender are at the heart of it, I also wanted to acknowledge that children like my daughter are part of a larger family web, and there are reverberations throughout. Siblings also need direction on how to support their new sibling's gender identity and may need some time to adjust.

Luckily, in our case, the adjustment happened. My children's relationship resolved, and it became clear that Rose—now Rosie—really was the same person, just with a new name and gender. Today, both of my kids are happy and confident in themselves and each other. They are proud to be part of a social group that understands that gender is a spectrum, that gender identity is self-determined, and that gender expression is something that can be played with and explored rather than dictated.

-Adria

For Oliver and Rosie,
as they were,
as they are,
and as they will be

Love, Mom

Published by Capstone Editions, an imprint of Capstone.
1710 Roe Crest Drive
North Mankato, Minnesota 56003
capstonepub.com

Text copyright © 2021 by Adria Karlsson.
Illustrations copyright © 2021 by Linus Curci.

Library of Congress Cataloging-in-Publication Data

Names: Karlsson, Adria, author. | Curci, Linus, illustrator.
Title: My sister, Daisy / by Adria Karlsson ; illustrations by Linus Curci.
Description: North Mankato, Minnesota : Capstone Editions, an imprint of Capstone, [2021] |
Audience: Ages 5–7. | Audience: Grades K–1. | Summary: An older brother reacts to his younger
sibling's gender transformation with compassion. Includes a note from the author.
Identifiers: LCCN 2021002338 (print) | LCCN 2021002339 (ebook) |
ISBN 9781684463848 (hardcover) | ISBN 9781684463817 (pdf) | ISBN 9781684463831 (kindle edition)
Subjects: CYAC: Brothers and sisters—Fiction. | Transgender people—Fiction.
Classification: LCC PZ7.1.K3545 My 2021 (print) | LCC PZ7.1.K3545 (ebook) | DDC [E]—dc23
LC record available at https://lccn.loc.gov/2021002338
LC ebook record available at https://lccn.loc.gov/2021002339

Designed by Nathan Gassman

Consultant Credits: Sabra L. Katz-Wise, PhD, Assistant Professor at Boston Children's Hospital,
Harvard Medical School, and the Harvard T. H. Chan School of Public Health